The Fairy Who Saved Christmas

Written by Aoife Lawler

Illustrated by Elisha Sophie Petticrew

Have you ever wondered how Santa fits down each and every chimney, big or small?

Well we know how – fairy dust!

This incredibly precious dust is found when the first light of dawn hits the frozen or snowy ground and creates a beautiful sparkle.

Each fairy places the sparkles they have collected into a hole in the Fairy Tree all throughout the winter. Then every Christmas Eve all of these sparkles come together to create a very magical dust called Iridescence.

Now what is also not so well known, is that it is the job of one particular group of fairies to bring the Iridescence to Santa's Gnome Sesil, on Christmas Eve just before dusk. This group of fairies have to be extra careful not to be seen in daylight because as we all know: if a human sees a fairy they lose a little of their magic.

This story is about one Christmas Eve when the Iridescence handover did not go so smoothly...

On that particular evening a group of fairies known as the Delivery Pack including a very excited young fairy called Pepper, flew to Santa's workshop and headed straight for the Delivery Room. While the other fairies stopped to catch their breath after their long flight carrying the big purse of Iridescence, Finn the Head Fairy knocked loudly on the door. The door swung open to reveal Sesil the Gnome.

Of course he was expecting them and acknowledged them with a simple nod of his head.

Pepper stared wide-eyed around the Delivery Room. This was her first journey as part of the Delivery Pack and she was absolutely thrilled to actually be in Santa's home!

"Thank you," said Sesil and Finn bowed. The fairies began to turn and follow Finn flying away. Pepper, totally in awe of being in Santa's house, took a moment to realise that it was time to go. She turned to catch up with the others but felt instantly that her flying was harder now and much slower.

Maybe she was just tired after the long flight?

"Stop!!!" Sesil's voice boomed through the night air.

Finn, Pepper and the rest of the Delivery Pack stopped suddenly and looked back. For a moment Pepper had no idea what was happening...

That was until she saw Finn's face. Something was very wrong.

She followed his gaze to a button on her own dress.

Pepper's dress button had somehow gotten caught up with a string from the Iridescence purse and caused it to unravel leaving the precious dust to sink into the snow beneath.

Pepper was horrified.
How could this have happened?

Finn flew straight back down to the door with Pepper and the rest of the Delivery Pack following him.

"She is new," Finn explained quietly.
"You'd better come with me," Sesil instructed.

Pepper watched as Finn followed
and the door closed behind them.
Pepper's heart was beating very fast and
she felt that she had stopped breathing!

What was going to happen now?

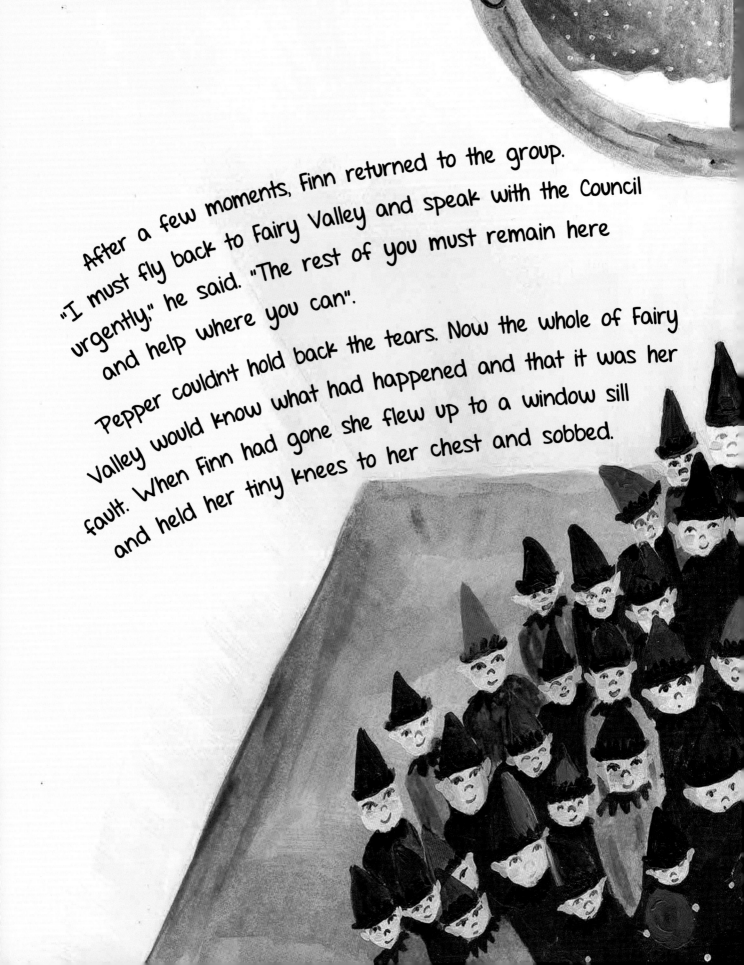

After a few moments, Finn returned to the group. "I must fly back to Fairy Valley and speak with the Council urgently," he said. "The rest of you must remain here and help where you can".

Pepper couldn't hold back the tears. Now the whole of Fairy Valley would know what had happened and that it was her fault. When Finn had gone she flew up to a window sill and held her tiny knees to her chest and sobbed.

Pepper sat there for a long time until a voice inside the house caught her attention. It was a voice she always longed to hear. Drying her tears she wiped a tiny panel in the window and peered inside.

There stood Santa himself with dozens and dozens of elves all around. Pepper glanced at their faces, they all looked worried. Her heart sank once more.

She sat back down and gazed ahead. The sun was setting and Pepper watched as soft sparkles bounced off the snow beneath.

"That's it!" she squealed and flew down to pick up a sparkle that had just settled on the snowy ground. As she picked it up she could feel its power in her tiny hand.

"Not as strong as a dawn sparkle, but maybe it could work?" she muttered to herself, her heart racing once more. She sped back to the other fairies and told them her idea. They immediately set to work gathering as many dusk sparkles as they could.

Pepper didn't waste any time and raced to the Delivery Room door and knocked as hard as she could. Sesil pulled it open and glared down at Pepper.

"What is it Pepper?" he barked.

"I have to speak to Santa," she said as bravely as she could. Sesil raised his eyebrow.

"Please, I need to show him this." She held out her tiny hand. The sparkle blinked up at them.

"You'd better come with me," Sesil sighed.

Sesil walked quickly through the gigantic home
with Pepper flying close behind him. They
passed hundreds if not thousands of
worried-looking elves. Eventually they came to a
huge red door and knocked once before opening
it. A sea of elves turned to look in their direction.

"What is it Sesil?" a warm voice asked.

"It's the fairy who lost the Iridescence Santa, she wants to
show you something," said Sesil.

Pepper could feel her face getting redder and redder.

"Show her in, then," Santa instructed. The sea of elves began to part, leaving a path for Pepper.

"By the way Sesil, that was a little harsh. It seems you have forgotten your first day here," Santa smiled.

"Come here little magical one" said Santa. Pepper slowly flew along the path the elves had made. She looked up as Santa tapped his arm. She flew up and landed on the softest, reddest velvet she had ever felt.

"There is no need to look so troubled, little one," he said gently.

"I have found something that might help," Pepper said and opened her hand to reveal the shimmering dusk sparkle.

"This is not Iridescence little one, what is it?" Santa asked.

"It's a sparkle from dusk, just as the sun set this evening, Santa. I can feel its power but I'm not sure if it is as powerful as a dawn sparkle. Maybe it won't be strong enough to magically transport you and the gifts down the chimney, but it can do this."

Pepper flew over and landed beside a wrapped parcel and blew the tiny sparkle towards it. Pepper watched as the sparkle danced towards the parcel and landed gently on it. She closed her eyes and wished as hard as she could.

When she opened her eyes she saw the sparkle burst into a thousand pieces and fall like rain across the parcel before it disappeared. Pepper flew back over to where Santa was sitting with the trail of shimmering dust floating behind her.

"I'm fairly sure that each sparkle will be strong enough to transport the allocated presents into each home. The only problem is that it may not be strong enough to transport you down the chimney too," said Pepper.

"There is just one more thing... The sparkle will only follow fairy magic so each present must be led into the house by a fairy." Pepper held her breath and searched Santa's big face to see any sign of his approval.

Suddenly, a great big smile spread across Santa's face.
"The little fairy who lost the Iridescence has saved Christmas!
What is your name little one?" asked Santa.
"It's Pepper," said Pepper excitedly.

"Hooray for Pepper!" Santa's voice boomed
and the room rejoiced.

"Stations everyone! Children need their presents and we
are already behind," he instructed. All the elves ran in
every direction, talking excitedly to one another.

Santa stood up from his chair and put his hands on his gigantic hips.
"Oscar," he called and an important-looking elf walked quickly over.

"Send the Owls to Fairy Valley and tell them what little
Pepper here has discovered and ask my good friend
Queen Kate to rally her troops."

0
Days left until
Christmas.

"Tell her to make sure that every fairy living with a human family knows that they must help deliver their family's toys."

"But Santa, not every home has a house fairy," Pepper interjected. Santa turned to look at her. "Don't they? How odd."

He paused and rubbed his beard for a moment.

"Perhaps the National Fairy Council should alert all the fairies around the world whether they are house fairies or not. Ask that everyone go to Fairy Valley to collect their dusk sparkle and meet you at each house. Then that way those who don't already have a house fairy will get their presents delivered too."

"We really must act quickly though!" said Pepper.

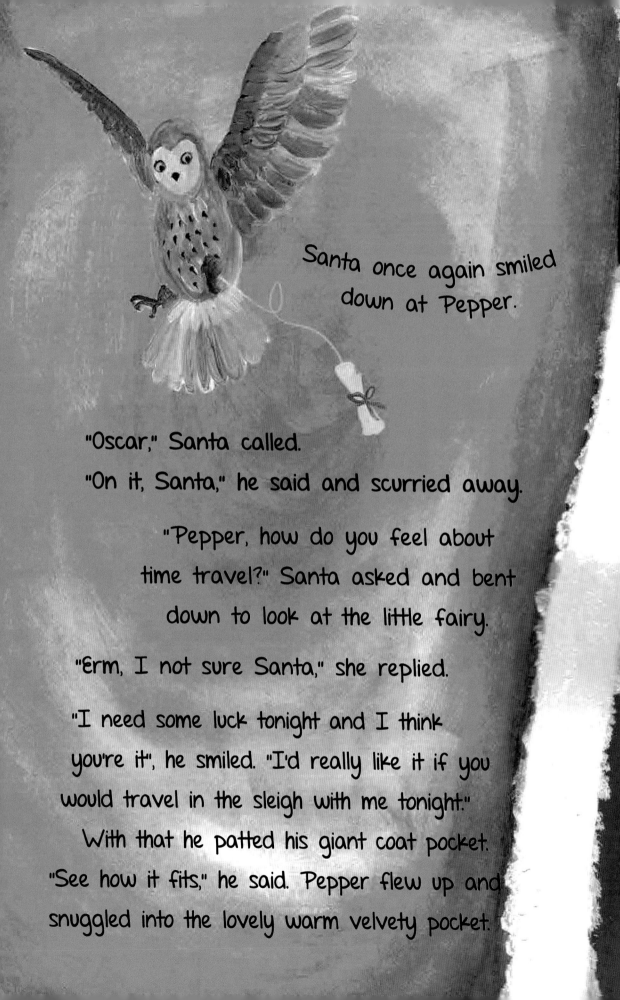

Santa once again smiled
down at Pepper.

"Oscar," Santa called.
"On it, Santa," he said and scurried away.

"Pepper, how do you feel about
time travel?" Santa asked and bent
down to look at the little fairy.

"Erm, I not sure Santa," she replied.

"I need some luck tonight and I think
you're it", he smiled. "I'd really like it if you
would travel in the sleigh with me tonight."
With that he patted his giant coat pocket.
"See how it fits," he said. Pepper flew up and
snuggled into the lovely warm velvety pocket.

"You fit perfectly. Lets do this together. We make a great team!" said Santa.
Pepper looked uncertain.
"Are you sure? I messed up before, I could mess it up again," she said.

Santa smiled. "Pepper it was an accident. Everyone makes mistakes. And anyway, haven't you solved the problem? Your clever discovery has saved Christmas!"

For the first time that day Pepper breathed a sigh of relief. She knew however that it was a big ask to get all of the fairies organised in time and worried that Queen Kate and the Council may not forgive her as easily.

Meanwhile back in Fairy Valley, the news had reached Queen Kate and she was busy organising all of fairy-kind to help Santa on the most important night of the year.

It had worked because when Santa's sleigh arrived at the first house a fairy stood eagerly on the chimney top. Time after time Pepper would show the fairies what to do. Each one of them would use the sparkle they had collected and transport the presents into the house. Santa would tell them where to place the presents after checking his lists.

Santa stopped his sleigh. "Last 20,000 houses Pepper, maybe you could do one yourself. What do you think?"

Pepper did not feel like she deserved to deliver any presents. She almost ruined Christmas for the entire world. On one of the last roof tops, Pepper flew up to find no fairy there standing by the chimney.

"Oh no!" she gasped as Santa climbed up beside her. He looked around anxiously and then suddenly his face broke out into a happy smile once again. "Not to worry Pepper – here she is."

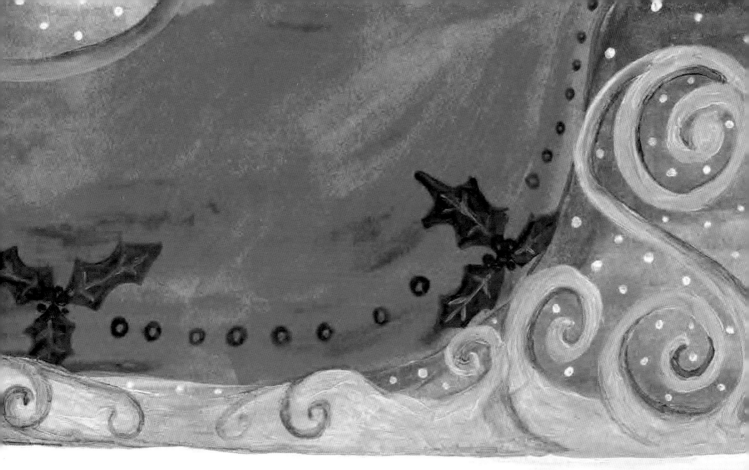

Pepper followed his gaze and watched as a bright golden glow appeared to be coming from just under the rooftop. With that, Queen Kate herself flew up onto the chimney and landed just beside Santa.

"Ah hello there Kate, so good to see you again," he said.

"Hi Santa, you're looking well!" said Queen Kate with a beautiful smile. She turned to look at Pepper.

"Pepper," she said and Pepper could feel her lip start to quiver and her eyes fill with tears. "How can we ever thank you?" asked Queen Kate.

"Thank me?" Pepper said, her eyes wide with disbelief.

"Why yes, you have saved Christmas!"
said Queen Kate. "But I lost the entire year's worth of
Iridescence first," Pepper said quietly.

Queen Kate went over to Pepper and held her hand tightly.

"You are as you should be, clever, creative and hard working.
You made a mistake but you also made it right again. I am
so very proud of you," said Queen Kate hugging Pepper tightly.

"Right then Kate, let's finish this job. Off you go!" said Santa.
"I think Pepper should deliver these presents," she said and
held out her hand to reveal a beautiful dusk sparkle.

"Oh Queen Kate, are you sure?" Pepper asked.

"I believe in you,"
Queen Kate said.

"I believe in you too,"
said Santa.

"Thank you so much. Here goes!" said Pepper.
With that she disappeared down the chimney with the dust sparkle tightly in her hand.

That Christmas was a resounding success!

Every child woke up to find their gifts had been delivered and every fairy celebrated their new hero –

Pepper, the fairy who saved Christmas!

The End